They open the front door. Inside, they see an old winding staircase.

Upstairs, Brother looks for Gracie. "Yikes!" he says. "There's someone in here!"

"It's just a mirror," says Sister. "Maybe
Gracie is behind it. Whoops! I guess not!"

Inside the bedroom, Sister looks for
Gracie in a cupboard. "Uh-oh!" she says.
"Gracie doesn't have four eyes!"

"What's behind this curtain?" wonders Brother. "Hmm! She doesn't look very friendly. Let's get out of here!"

"Is Gracie behind this very small door?"
says Sister. "Oh, dear! Excuse me!"

"Maybe she's behind this big door," says Brother.

"These suits of armor sound hollow," Sister says, knocking on one. "Is anyone home?"

"Maybe Gracie climbed inside one of these," says Brother. "Let's take a look."

"This must be the library," says Sister. "I wonder what this book is. Oh, it's *Frankenbear!*"

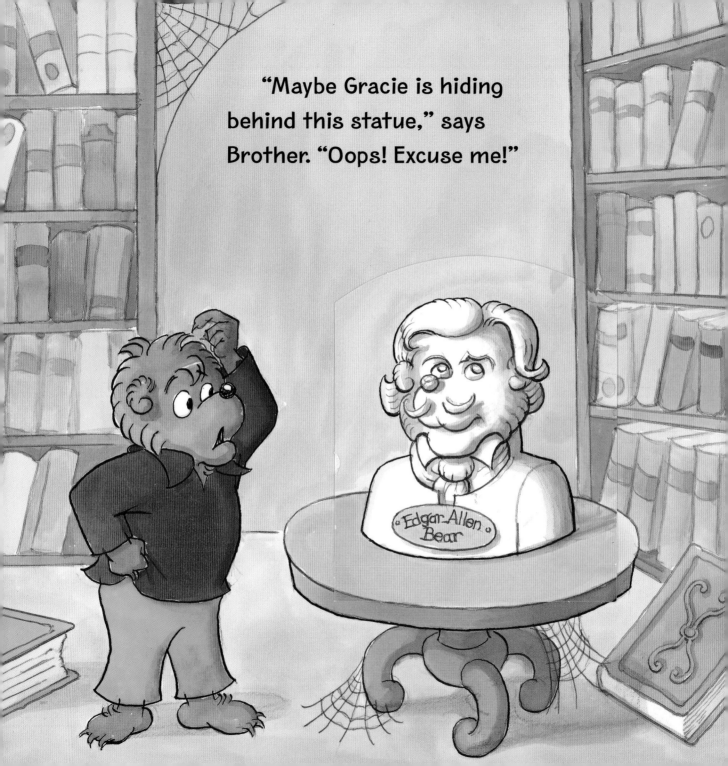

Brother and Sister go into another room. Is
Gracie behind this chair? Hooray! Here she is! But
someone else is here, too.

"Welcome to my home!" says Missus Grizzus.
"Would you like some pumpkin pie?"